THE PATH

박
노
해
사
진
에
세
이

03

길

THE PATH

PARK NOHAE PHOTO ESSAY 03

느린걸음

길을 잃으면 길이 찾아온다
길을 걸으면 길이 시작된다
길은 걷는 자의 것이니

If you lose your way, the path will find you
If you start to walk, the path will begin
The path belongs to the walker

CONTENTS

길은 걷는 자의 것이다

길을 보면 눈물이 난다. 누군가 처음 걸었던 길 없는 길. 여러 사람이 걷고 걸어 길이 된 길. 그 길 하나를 만들기 위해 앞서 걷다 쓰러져간 사람들. 자신의 흰 뼈를 이정표로 세워두고 바람처럼 구름처럼 떠나간 사람들. 길을 걸으면 그 발자국 소리가 울린다.

우리 모두는 길 위의 사람들. 길은, 인간人間의 길이다. 인생이란 끝없이 갈라지는 두 갈래 길에서 고뇌하고 결단하는 선택의 연속이다. 그리하여 내가 걷는 그 길을 따라 하루하루 달라져 가는 쉬임 없는 생성의 존재가 나, 인간이다.

그럼에도 나는 탄생의 순간 이미 나다. 누구라도 이 지구별에 목숨 받고 태어난 날, 이번 생에 꼭 해야만 할 소명召命이 있어 자기 운명의 길 하나 품고 나오지 않았던가. 이 우주 역사에서 단 하나뿐이고 단 한 번뿐인 내 인생의 이유와 의미를 묻고 찾아가는 것, 그것이 '인간의 길'이 아닌가.

아, 그러나 슬프게도 우리는 길을 잃어버렸다. 인류가 탄생한 이

래 가장 많은 지식이 흘러 다니고 세계와 실시간으로 소통하고 지구 끝까지 길이 이어졌으나, 정작 자신이 가야 할 길은 잃어버렸다. 나는 나 자신과 가장 먼 자가 되어버렸다. 나는 나에게 가장 낯선 자가 되어버렸다. 이것이 지금 세상에서 가장 중대한 사건이다.

나는 고아, 우주의 고아. 길을 잃고 밤마다 꿈길을 걸어오는 내가 있다. 내 안의 나를 부르는 소리를 잊어버리기 위해 끝없는 중독과 도피와 마취가 아니면 불안과 공허로 견딜 수 없는 시대. 내가 정말로 무얼 원하는지도 모른 채 끝없이 원하고, '나 어떻게 살아야 하나'를 모른 채 무엇을 더해야 할까 찾아다니고, '어떤 내가 되어야 하나'를 모른 채 타인의 시선과 인정을 갈망하고 있다.

세상에서 가장 괴롭고 비참한 자는 길을 잃어버린 자다. 길을 잃고 나를 잃고 희망이 없는 자다. 우리가 길을 잃어버린 것은 길이 사라져 버려서가 아니다. 너무 많은 길이 나 있기 때문이다. 우리가 앞이 보이지 않는 것은 어둠이 깊어져서가 아니다. 너무 현란한 빛에 눈이 멀어서이다. 우리가 희망이 없다는 것은 희망을 찾지 못해서가 아니다. 너무 헛된 희망을 놓지 못해서이다.

그리하여 길을 잃은 사람들이 몰려가는 곳이 길이 되고 말았다. 다들 가니까 그 길로 달려가고, 다들 가는 그 길을 앞서가고자 비교 경쟁하고 인정 투쟁하고, 잠깐 흘러 가버리는 유행과 팔림에 휩쓸려 갈 때, 길은 나를 지나쳐 버린다. 나는 나를 지나쳐 버린다.

2020년 오늘, 세계가 재난 상황이라 한다. 재난disaster의 어원은 '떨어지다'라는 뜻의 dis와 '별'이라는 뜻의 astro가 합쳐진 '별이 떨어진 상태', '별이 없는 상태'를 가리킨다. 저 밤하늘의 별처럼 글썽이며 빛나던 나 자신과의 내적 연결이 끊어지고, 어둠 속 별의 지도와도 같던 성현과 스승과 시인과 탐험가와 수도자와 혁명가들이 떨어져 나간 세계. 그리하여 지구 중력권과 나 자신에게 갇혀버린 상태. 더는 나아갈 길이 없고 희망이 없는 처지가 재난disaster이다.

코로나19 사태로 세상이 일제히 멈추고 인간의 길이 끊긴 지금. 역사상 처음으로 78억 지구 인간이 동시에 공포에 휩싸인 강렬한 체험. 실시간으로 목도한 세상 끝의 풍경. '불가촉 세계'의 날들. 지구 인류가 하나로 촘촘히 이어진 이 문명의 정점에서 인간의 길을 잃어버린 대재난의 상황이다.

우리 인간은 위대한 여정Great Journey으로부터 사막과 고원과 동토를 걸어 여기까지 왔다. 길을 가면서 새로운 길이 만들어졌고 길이 이어져 하나가 되어갔다. 길 위에서 사상이 탄생하고 사건이 벌어지고 사물을 창출했다. 그렇게 길을 걸으며 만나고 함께하고, 살고 살게 하고, 사랑하고 잉태하고, 더 커진 나로 진보해왔다.

인류의 역사는 '접촉의 역사'다. 만남과 대화, 포옹과 사랑 없이 인류는 존재할 수도 진보할 수도 없다. 인간의 진보란 더 낯설고 다양한 존재와의 접촉의 확대를 통해 이루어진 것이다. 경계와 두려움, 손해와 죽음까지를 감수하고 낯선 이들과 기꺼이 접촉하고 받아들이는 결단과 용기, 인간의 길을 끊고 막는 자들에 맞선 저항과 모험. 우리는 그것을 사랑과 자비, 선과 정의, 우애와 환대라 불러왔다. 인간성의 절정인 사랑은, 위험을 무릅쓴 '끌어안음'이고 너에게로의 '투신'인 것이다.

그런데 우리는 지금 '인간성의 대변형'을 겪고 있다. 서로가 만나고 모이고 나누고 해내며 살아온 사람과 사람 사이, 그 인간人間의 길이 끊겨버렸다. 사람이 사람에게 공포가 되고, 조금의 위험과 손해도

거리두기로 차단해야 한다는 의식이 전염병처럼 번져가고 있다. '접촉의 역사'로부터 역행하는 것은 '사랑의 감축'이고 사랑의 소멸이라는 비상사태의 징표이기도 하다.

'포스트 코로나'를 말하고 '이 또한 지나가리라' 말하지만 '코로나 이후'란 없다. 코로나 이후는 더 독한, 더 잦은, 더 다른 코로나의 시대일 것이다. 언젠가는 코로나 저편의 검은 그림자가 드러나리라. 지금 인류는 일제히 마스크를 낀 '묵언수행' 중이고, 자발적 강제로 문을 닫아건 '방안거' 중이다. 그럼에도 코로나 시대 안에서 우리는 길을 걸어야만 한다. 더 속 깊은 만남으로 나누고 모이고 얼굴을 마주 보며 생생히 살아야 한다. 지구 인류 문명의 정점에서 기습당한 코로나 시대를 기회 삼아, 새로운 철학과 삶의 양식을 찾는 길로 나아가야 하고, 이 재난 사태를 낭비하지 않고 '더 나아지는 나'로 도약해야 한다.

자기 시대의 진실을 보기 원한다면 멀리서, 거슬러 올라가 봐야 한다. 완전히 다른 세계의 시간으로 거슬러 오를 때, 현재로부터의 거리가 확보될 때, 그리하여 과거를 다 삼킨 시대의 높이에 설 때, 오늘의 세계가 가는 방향이 보인다. 오늘의 사회로부터 '얼마나 멀리 떨어져 있을 수 있는가' 그것이 길을 찾는 사람의 진정한 능력이다.

나는 가능한 가장 오래된 시간, 가장 오래된 장소, 가장 오래된 사람 속으로 걸어 들어가 '앞선 과거'로 돌아 나오는 길을 찾아 나섰다. 인간의 길은 눈앞에서 보면 직선이지만 멀고 크고 높은 곳에서 보면 동그란 길이기에.

세계 어느 도시나 똑같아진 이 '평평한 세계'의 삶의 방식과 유행과 우리 시대의 확실성으로부터 나 자신을 가장 멀리 떨어지게 하여,

두 세계의 공간과 시간 사이의 여정에 대한 감각을 회복하고, 무디어진 나의 인간적 감각을 되살리고자 했다.

하여 나는 지상의 가장 멀고 높고 깊은 곳을 찾아다니며 오래된 토박이들이 지켜온 인간의 길을 탐구하고 경청하고 담아왔다. 우리가 앞만 보고 달리다 놓쳐온 것, 진보했으나 결핍된 것, 무언가 온전하고 올바른 것, 잃어버린 시원의 순수, 수만 년 이어온 희망의 씨앗을 찾아 헤맸다. 우리에게 사라진 그 원형질을 품고 돌아 나와 진보한 오늘의 우리 안에서 새로이 살려내는 여명의 길 하나 찾고 싶었다. 그것이 살아남은 혁명가의 사명이라 생각하며 나를 내몰았다.

그러나 길 찾는 나의 유랑길은 '길을 잃는 일'이었다. 나는 기꺼이 길을 잃어버렸고, 비틀거리며 길을 헤맸다. 길을 잃어버리자 길이 내게로 걸어왔다.

길을 잃어보았나. 몇 번이나 길을 잃어보았나. 여행길에서 길을 잃어보았나. 사랑 안에서 길을 잃어보았나. 일상 속에서 길을 잃어보았나. 신념 속에서 길을 잃어보았나. 그때, 길을 잃어버린 그 막막함 속에서 무엇이 찾아오던가. 여정의 놀라움이, 느닷없는 마주침이, 전혀 새로운 길이, 불꽃의 만남이, 또 다른 내가 마주 걸어오지 않던가.

우리가 세워야 할 것은 계획이 아니다. 먼저 세워야 할 것은 내 삶의 목적지다. '나 어떻게 살아서는 안 되는가'에 대한 확고한 원칙이다. 내가 결코 놓지 말아야 할 나의 첫마음, 그 첫마음의 불빛은 내 생의 최종 목적지에 놓여 나를 비추고 있고, 내가 가야만 할 길을 가리키고 있다. 나머지는 다 '여정의 놀라움'과 '인연의 신비'에 맡겨두기로 하자. '계획의 틈새'와 '비움의 여백' 사이로 걸어올 나만의 다른 길을 위해.

하나의 길이 끝나는 곳에서 길은 반드시 다시 열린다. 주어진 길 밖의 모든 길들이 그대의 것이다. 심어진 꿈 밖의 모든 꿈들이 그대의 것이다. 길을 잃고 길을 찾는 그 발길들이 세상의 판을 흔든다.

그러니 길을 잘못 들어섰다고 슬퍼하지 마라, 포기하지 마라. 삶에서 잘못 들어선 길이란 없으니. 모든 새로운 길이란 잘못 들어선 발길에서 찾아졌으니. 나만의 빛나는 길은 잘못 내디딘 발자국들로 인하여 비로소 찾아지고 길이 되는 것이니.

이 지상에 나는 단 하나뿐이듯 진정한 나의 길은 하나뿐인 길이다. 비교 경쟁할 수 없는 나만의 길, 진정한 자신을 사는 용기, 우리에겐 지금 '결정적 한 걸음'이 필요하다. 수많은 경험을 소유해도, 백 걸음 만 걸음을 앞서가도, 결정적 한 걸음이 없이는 다 헛된 진보이다. 수많은 걱정과 불안도 수많은 문제와 대책도 결정적 한 걸음으로 정리되고 소멸된다.

팽팽히 당겨진 활시위처럼 삶의 목적을 향해 온 존재를 정렬시킨 결정적 한 걸음을 내딛을 때, 자신의 두 발로 인생의 대지를 걸어가는 한 인간이, 진정한 인간이 탄생하는 것이다. 그 순간 세계에 고요한 파동이 일고 거기 이어진 인간의 마음으로 공명된다고 나는 믿는다.

지구의 중력에 맞서 직립한 인간, 이 불편하고 비효율이고 갖은 질병을 가져오는 직립보행의 인간 종. 직립한 인간의 두 발은 두 길을 동시에 걷는다. 함께 가는 길 속에서 나만의 다른 길을. 밖으로 펼쳐가는 운동 속에서 안으로 걸어드는 운동을. 오래된 길을 거슬러 새로운 여명의 길을. 지상의 길로 한 걸음 걸으며 하늘로 오르는 한 걸음을. 그리하여 길은 세상에 있으나 이미 내 안에 있는 길이 아닌가.

돌아보면 이미 먼지처럼 사라진 내 발자국, 내가 걸어온 길들에 남은 건 눈물 어린 사랑뿐이다. 그러나 아직 길은 끝나지 않았고 내 발은 아직 다 닳지 않았으니. 나에겐 가야만 할 길이 있고 찾아야만 할 무언가가 있으니. 나는 먼 곳으로, 더 먼 곳으로, 더 깊고 먼 곳으로, 다시 길 없는 길을 떠나는 것이다.

　　무엇이 이토록 지친 나를 걷게 하는가. 사랑만이 나를 다시 걷게 한다. 나는 사랑 안에서 나를 잃어버린다. 사랑 안에서 길을 잃어버린다. 그러면 사랑이 어디론가 나를 데려다주리라. 나를 향해 마주 걸어오고 있는 너에게로, 아직 내가 모르는 내 안의 또 다른 나에게로.

　　먼 길을 걸어온 사람아
　　아무것도 두려워 마라.
　　그대는 충분히 고통받아왔고
　　그래도 우리는 여기까지 왔다.
　　자신을 잃지 마라.
　　믿음을 잃지 마라.
　　걸어라. 너만의 길로 걸어가라.
　　길은 걷는 자의 것이다.
　　길을 걸으면 길이 시작된다.

2020년 9월
박노해

The path belongs to the walker

At the sight of the path, tears begin to flow. A path without a path that someone walks along for the first time. A path that became a path when many people had walked along it. The people who walked ahead and fell, in order to make that one path. The people who left their white bones as signposts then left like the wind, like clouds. Their footsteps ring out when you walk along the path.

We are all people on paths. The path is the path of human life. Life is a series of choices that are agonized over and decided on before an endless series of diverging paths. Therefore, depending on the path I take, I am, each human person is, a being in unceasing creation, changing day by day.

Nevertheless, I am already who I am at the moment of my birth. Surely, on the day that each one of us is born onto this global stage, we have a vocation we have to accomplish in this life, so that we each emerge embracing one destined path. Isn't that the "human path," asking about and seeking the reason and meaning of my life, which is unique, and occurs only once in cosmic history?

Oh, but sad to say, we have lost our way. Since the birth of mankind, the most knowledge went flowing, communicated to the world in real time, and the path reached to the ends of the earth, but at the same time we lost sight of the path we should take. I have become the person most remote from myself. I have become my own most total stranger. This is the most significant event in today's world.

I am an orphan, an orphan of the universe. There is an I that has lost its way and comes walking down dream-paths every night. An unbearable age with, in order to forget the voice calling me from inside, either endless addiction, flight and anesthesia, or anxiety and emptiness. Wanting endlessly, without knowing what I really want, seeking what more I should do without knowing how I should live, longing for attention and recognition from others without knowing what kind of person I should become.

The most anguished and wretched person in the world is one who has lost the way, one who has lost the path, lost himself or herself, without hope. If we have lost our way, it is not because the path has vanished. It is because there are too many paths. If we cannot see ahead, it is not because the darkness has grown deeper. Our eyes are blinded by too bright a light. If we have no hope, it is not because we cannot find hope. It is because we have failed to let go of false hopes.

Thus, the place where people who had lost their way crowded together became a path. As everyone takes it, goes hastening along that path, all intent on being in the lead along that path, competing in comparison, struggling for recognition, as they are swept away by fleeting fashions and sales, the path passes by me. I pass by myself.

2020, today, the world is said to be facing a disaster. The origin of the word *disaster*, which is a combination of *dis* which means 'fallen', and *astro*, which means 'star', refers to 'a state where a star has fallen' or 'a state without a star.' A world in which the inner connection with myself, bright and tearfully shining like a star in the night sky, has been broken, a world from which sages, teachers, poets, explorers, monks, and the revolutionaries, who were like maps of the stars in the dark, have fallen away. I am trapped in the Earth's gravitational sphere and myself. That state in which there is no path to continue along, no hope, is a *disaster.*

Now because of Covid-19 the whole world has come to a stop, humanity's paths have been cut. For the first time in history, an intense experience, 7.8 billion humans experiencing terror at the same time. A scene of the end of the world in real-time. Days of the 'Untouchable World'. It is a situation of great disaster that has lost the human path at this peak of civilization where the humanity of the earth was so closely connected.

We humans have traveled here in a *Great Journey* across deserts, plateaus and tundra. Advancing along the path, new paths were created and the paths joined to become one. On the path, ideas were born, events occurred, and objects were created. Walking along the path, we met, joined together, lived and brought to life, loved, conceived, and progressed toward a greater self.

The history of mankind is 'a history of contact'. Mankind cannot exist or progress without encounters, conversations, embraces, and love. Human progress has been made by expanding contact with more unfamiliar and diverse beings. Determination and courage to accept borders and fears, damage and deaths, a willingness to contact and accept strangers, resistance and adventure against those who break and stop human paths. We have called such things love and mercy, goodness and justice, friendship and hospitality. Love, which is the culmination of humanity, is an 'embrace' daring to risk, a 'commitment' to you.

However, we are now experiencing a 'great transformation of humanity'. The path between humans and humans, who have lived meeting, gathering, sharing together, has been cut. A consciousness that one person is a cause of fear to another and even a little danger and damage, must be kept away by distancing, is spreading like an epidemic. Retrogression from the 'history of contact' is a 'reduction of love' and also a sign of a state of emergency which is an annihilation of love.

People talk of 'post corona' and say 'this will also pass', but there is no 'after corona'. After this corona, there will be stronger, more frequent, and different corona eras. One day, the black shadow beyond corona will be revealed. Now, human beings all together are like Buddhist monks keeping "strict silence" in masks and they are in "enclosed retreat," voluntarily shutting their doors. Nevertheless, in the corona era, we have to keep following the path. We have to encounter from the deeper ground of our hearts, share and gather face to face and live vividly. At the peak of human civilization on the planet, we must take the opportunity of the corona era, and go forward to find a new philosophy and way of life.

If we want to see the truth of our times, we have to go back up, see from a distance. When we go back to a completely different world's time, when a distance from the present is secured, and therefore we stand at the height of the era that has fully swallowed up the past, we can see the direction today's world is taking. "How far away I can get" from today's society is the true ability of those who seek their path.

I walked into the oldest times, the oldest places, the oldest people I could find, looking for a path leading back to a 'precedent past'. The human path is straight when viewed from the front, but seen from a distant, vast and high place the path is circular.

Removing myself as far as possible from the ways of living, the fashions, the certainties of this "flat earth," which had become the same in every city in the world, I restored my sense of the journey between space and time in the two worlds, hoping to revive my faded human senses.

Thus, I have been searching, listening, capturing the human paths that the old natives have tended, visiting the most remote, high, and deep places on earth. I wandered in search of the things we had lost sight of while running ahead, something advanced but lacking, something complete and correct, the purity of the lost origins, the seeds of hope that have been transmitted over tens of thousands of years. I wanted to come back bringing the protoplasm that has disappeared from among us and find the path of a new dawn coming alive within us in our advanced today. I drove myself on, convinced it was the true mission of a surviving revolutionary.

However, my wandering in search of the path meant 'losing my way'. I lost my way willingly, stumbled, wandered. And whenever I lost my way, the path came toward me.

Have you lost your way? How many times have you lost your way? Have you ever lost your way on a journey? Have you ever lost your way in love? Have you lost your way in daily life? Have you lost your way in belief? At that moment, in the boundlessness of losing your way, what came to you? Was it not the surprise of a journey, an unexpected encounter, a completely new path, a pyrotechnic meeting, another I that came walking toward you?

What we have to establish is not a plan. The first thing to be established is my life's destination. It's a firm principle about how I ought not to live. My first heart that I should never let go of, the light of that first heart is at the final destination of my life, illuminating me and pointing out the path I must take. Let's leave the rest to 'the surprise of the journey' and the 'mystery of relationship.' For the sake of my own other path that will come walking between the 'gaps in plans' and 'the blank of emptiness.'

Where one path ends, another path is sure to open. All paths outside the given path are yours. All dreams outside already planted dreams are yours. The steps taken while getting lost and finding a path shake the world's boards.

Don't be sad, don't give up because you've taken the wrong path. In life there is no wrong path. Every new path is found by taking steps along the wrong path. My own shining path is found and becomes my path only by wrong steps.

Just as I am unique on this earth, there is only one true path for me. My own path, one that cannot be compared in competition with others, the courage to live my true selfhood, we need 'a decisive step' now. Even possessing much experience, even after moving a hundred steps, ten thousand steps forward, it is all in vain without one decisive step. Numerous anxieties, uncertainties, numerous problems and countermeasures are cleared up and destroyed by one decisive step.

When one takes a decisive step that aligns one's whole being with the purpose of life, like a tightly drawn bowstring, a human being walking across the ground of his life with his own two feet, a true person, is born. At that moment, I believe that there a tranquil wave rises in the world and resonates with the human heart linked to it.

Human beings stand upright despite the Earth's gravity, this human species walking upright despite the discomfort, the inefficiency, the various diseases. The two feet of the upright human person walk on two paths simultaneously. A different path of my own within the path we go along together. Within a movement spreading outward, a movement walking inward. The path of a new dawn ascending to an old path. Advancing one step along a path on the ground and one step into the sky. So it seems that the road is in the world, but it is already within me.

Looking back, my footprints have already disappeared like dust, and the only thing left on the paths I've been walking along is tearful love. But the path has not ended yet, and my feet are not completely worn out yet. I have a path to take and something to look for. I am setting off again along a pathless path, farther, farther, deeper and farther.

What makes me keep walking though I am exhausted? Only love makes me keep walking. I lose myself in love. I lose my way in love. Then love will take me somewhere. Toward you who come walking towards me, toward another self inside of me that I don't know as yet.

You who have walked a long way along the path
fear nothing.
You have suffered enough along the way
yet nonetheless, we have reached here.
Do not lose yourself.
Do not lose faith.
Keep walking. Walk along your own path.
The path belongs to the walker.
If you start to walk, the path will begin.

September, 2020
Park Nohae

하 늘 까 지 이 어 진 밭

'하늘까지 이어진 밭'이라 불리는 '안데스' 고원.
만년설산의 흰 기침이 선득 이마에 닿는 아침,
눈바람 사이로 눈부신 태양이 길을 비춘다.
지구의 저 높고 험준한 고원에서 차빈Chavin 문명과
나스카Nazca 문명 그리고 잉카Inca 문명을 일군 사람들.
수천 년 된 안데스의 고원 길을 걸어갈 때
맨발로 이 길을 내어온 발자국 소리가 울린다.
지상의 무거운 중력을 이고 지고 걸어 오르는
안데스 농부들의 하늘 걸음이 울려온다.

A FIELD REACHING THE SKY

The Andes Plateau is known as 'a field reaching the sky.' On mornings when
the white cough of eternally snow-covered mountains touches chill brows,
dazzling sunlight shines down on the paths between flurries of snow.
On Earth's high, rugged plateau, people once cultivated the Chavin civilization,
the Nazca civilization, the Inca civilization. Walking along the paths of
the Andes Plateau, thousands of years old, the sound of the bare feet that once
walked along the paths resonates. The steps resonate of Andean peasants
walking skyward, bearing the ground's heavy gravity on their heads and backs.

On the way to Pisac village, Andes Mts., Peru, 2010.

차마고도의 석두성

'구름의 남쪽' 윈난雲南의 숨은 보석인 석두성은
거대한 암석 지반에 세워진 높다란 마을이다.
그 옛날 티베트의 말과 윈난성, 쓰촨성의 차를
교역하며 만들어진 차마고도茶馬古道는
실크로드보다 앞선 인류의 가장 오래된 문명 길이다.
오로지 말과 사람의 두 발로만 들어갈 수 있는 길.
석두성 마을의 여인이 가파른 비탈에 쌓아 올린
계단밭에서 기른 작물을 담아 장터로 나선다.

SHITOUCHENG ON THE ANCIENT TEA ROUTE

Shitoucheng, the hidden gem of Yunnan, 'the South of the clouds,' is a high-up village built in a region full of large stones. The Ancient Tea Route, constructed for an exchange of trade, horses from Tibet, tea from Yunnan and Sichuan, is the oldest road of human civilization, older than the Silk Road. A path that can only be taken by horses and human feet. A woman from Shitoucheng Village carries to market crops grown on the terraced fields built on the steep slopes.

Shitoucheng, Yunnan, China, 2007.

A BORDER RIVER

This river is a border. The Moei River traverses Thailand and Burma. Because of long military dictatorship and civil war, it's home for refugees driven out of Burma, a border river stained with the blood and tears of democratic youth and tribal minorities' liberation armies. The singing of Karen refugee women on their way home after doing laundry flows like a river and melts the tension of the border. "We laugh when life is difficult and when life is good." Can they be poor if they laugh despite being poor? Can they be deprived of human affection, even if they suffer?

Maesot, Thailand, 2011.

국 경 의 강

이 강이 국경이다.

타이와 버마를 가로지르며 흐르는 모에이 강.

오랜 군부독재와 내전으로

버마에서 쫓겨나온 난민들의 삶터이자

민주 청년들과 소수민족 해방군의

피와 눈물이 흐르는 국경의 강.

빨래를 하고 집으로 돌아가는

카렌족 난민 여인들의 노랫소리가

강물처럼 흐르며 국경의 긴장을 녹인다.

"어려울 때도 좋을 때도 우리는 웃음 지어요."

가난하다고 웃음마저 가난하겠는가.

고난이라고 인정마저 빼앗기겠는가.

등 뒤의 그대가 있어

화산 폭발로 생겨난 비옥한 대지에서 자라는

인도네시아의 과일과 야채는 그 맛이 일품이다.

수확한 과일을 지고 나서는 아빠를 배웅하는 가족.

이것이 고단한 노동 속에서도 내가 사는 힘이다.

내 등 뒤에 그대가 있어 나는 나아갈 수 있으니.

나는 나 하나만의 존재가 아니다.

내 힘만으로 살아가는 생이 아니다.

내 등 뒤를 지켜주는 이들이 있어

그래도 나는 살아갈 것이니.

I HAVE YOU BEHIND MY BACK

Growing on the fertile ground created by volcanic eruptions, Indonesia's fruits and vegetables taste wonderful. A family sees off father carrying the fruit they have harvested. This is the power I live by even amidst hard work. I have you behind my back so I can move ahead. I am not someone existing alone. I am not living by my own strength alone. Since there are those who protect my back I can go on living.

Pakel village, Probolinggo, East Java, Indonesia, 2013.

CARRYING SNACKS

Indonesian farmers plant early rice, having created terraced rice fields by cutting the hillsides and compacting the soil, using only buffalos and human hands. When the splashing footsteps of a woman carrying snacks ring out, it is time to gather in the shade of a palm tree and gain new strength. Contentment means having your feet plunged deep in the soil. If I'm dissatisfied, isn't it because I'm being swept away onto a path with my feet far from the ground, without life, without friendship?

Bandung, West Java, Indonesia, 2013.

새참을 들고

물소와 사람의 손으로만 산비탈을 깎고 찰흙을 다져
층층의 논을 창조해낸 인도네시아 농부들이 올벼를 심는다.
새참을 든 여인의 첨벙이는 발소리가 울리면
이제 곧 야자수 그늘에 모여 앉아 힘을 채우리라.
만족滿足이란 발이 흙 속에 가득히 안기는 것.
내가 지금 불만에 찬 것은 대지에서 멀어진 두 발로
삶이 없고 우정이 없는 길로 쏠려가서가 아닌가.

바닷가 마을의 담소

인도 베따꾼 항구 바닷가 마을 사람들은
아침에 고깃배가 들어오면 물고기를 나르며
하루 벌어 하루 먹는 가난한 형편이지만
마을 골목길 어디서나 이런 모습이다.
서로 모여서 이야기를 하고 서로 들어주고
뭐라도 나눠 먹고 힘든 일은 같이 풀어간다.
사람과 사람 사이, 인간人間의 길만 끊기지 않으면
우리는 만나고 모이고 해내며 살아간다.

CHATTING IN A SEASIDE VILLAGE

The people in the seaside village in the Indian port of Betakkun who help transport the fish when the fishing boats come in each morning earn just enough for that day's food, poor indeed, yet everywhere in the village's alleyways you can see them sitting together, talking and listening to each other, sharing everything we have, solving difficulties together. So long as the path between one person and another is not cut we live, meeting, gathering, and achieving.

Puri, Orissa, India, 2013.

흙 바 닥 놀 이 터

학교도 없고 책도 없고 장난감도 귀한 이곳에서
아이들은 흙바닥과 돌멩이 하나만 있으면
금세 가지가지 놀이를 만들어낸다.
아이들의 작고 신비로운 가슴 안에는
이미 모든 씨앗이 다 심겨져 있으니.
결여는 창조성을 꽃피우는 개척지이니.

A DIRT PLAYGROUND

Here, where there's no school, no books, and even toys are rare, if the
children have the bare ground and one stone, they soon invent various games.
For in children's tiny, mysterious hearts all the seeds are already planted.
Necessity is the mother of invention.

Dala, Yangon, Burma, 2011.

길 손 을 위 한 기 도

마을 길가의 푸른 나무 아래
길손을 위한 의자와 물을 놓아두는 할머니.
아침 목욕을 마치고 정精한 몸과 마음으로
오래된 나무 성전에 꽃을 바치고 기도를 한다.
"길손들의 안녕을 비는 기도이지요.
우리 모두가 인생이란 길의 여행자이니
길손들은 다 나의 자매형제가 아니겠소."

PRAYER FOR WAYFARERS

Under a green tree by the roadside in the village one old woman prepares
a chair and some water for wayfarers. After her morning bath, with a
clean body and mind she offers flowers and prays at the old tree shrine.
"It's a prayer for the well-being of wayfarers. We are all traveling along
the path of life so that every wayfarer is my sister, my brother, for sure."

Mandalay, Burma, 2011.

LAST PILGRIMAGE

The Tibetans live through three stages in life. In adolescence, they learn to
live diligently, then until they're middle-aged they have a family, care for their
children, and in old age, they return to God and advance toward the next life.
"I have reached my life's last pilgrimage as forehead, palms, knees and toes
touch the ground. When I fall and become one with the earth, the wild flowers
speak, when I rise and join my hands, the clouds in the sky speak. When I was
working and earning a living, I couldn't listen, but now in an empty heart
calm joy comes rising up. When my soul leaves my old body I pray that it will
become the wild flowers of the meadows, the wings of an eagle and will fly
serenely to the next life."

Langmusi, Amdo Tibet, 2012.

마 지 막 순 례 길

티베트인들은 인생의 세 단계를 살아간다.
청년기에는 열심히 살아가는 법을 배우고
장년기까진 가정을 이루어 아이를 돌보고
노년이 되면 신에 귀의해 다음 생을 향한다.
"내 생의 마지막 순례길을 오체투지로 왔다오.
엎드려 대지와 하나가 되면 들꽃이 말을 하고
일어서 합장하면 하늘 구름이 말을 한다오.
일하고 살림할 땐 미처 귀 기울이지 못했는데
텅 빈 마음에 고요한 환희심이 차오른다오.
내 영혼이 낡은 육신을 떠나면
초원의 들꽃이 되고 독수리의 날개가 되어
다음 생으로 유유히 날아가기를 기도한다오."

A RIVER IN THE TIBETAN GRASSLANDS

A crimson sunset falls over a river in the Ruoergai Grasslands, the Yellow River, that twists and turns nine times as it begins to flow. Tourists are busily taking pictures of the wonderful scenery, and a Tibetan woman who couldn't find one customer for a ride all day long offers her evening prayers with bent shoulders. The horse feels sorry for her so stays by her side silently. A story told by the twisting river. Life is a matter of keeping going, going on despite everything. Even if the winding path is long and bitter, it's a matter of keeping going, not hurrying, becoming one another's path and keeping going.

Jiu qu huang he di yi wan, Ruoergai, Amdo Tibet, 2012.

54

티 베 트 초 원 의 강

황하가 처음 몸을 틀어 아홉 번 굽이쳐 흐르는
루얼까이 초원의 강물 위에 붉은 석양이 내린다.
관광객들은 절경을 촬영하느라 분주한데,
종일 손님을 태우지 못한 티베트 여인이
무거운 어깨로 저녁 기도를 바친다.
말은 미안한지 가만가만 그 곁을 지킨다.
굽이굽이 흘러온 강이 전하는 이야기.
삶은 가는 것이다. 그래도 가는 것이다.
굽이 돌아가는 길이 멀고 쓰릴지라도
서둘지 말고 가는 것이다.
서로가 길이 되어 가는 것이다.

브로모 화산의 농부

화산火山의 나라 인도네시아에서도
가장 웅장하고 아름다운 브로모 화산.
눈부신 운무 사이로 칼데라의 아침이 열리고
브로모의 농부는 대지에 뿌리박은 삶의
당당한 걸음으로 저 높은 밭으로 향한다.
누구도 무시하지 않고 무엇에도 꺾이지 않는
인간의 등뼈를 곧게 세우고 세상을 걸어간다.

FARMERS OF MOUNT BROMO

Even in Indonesia, the land of volcanoes, the most magnificent and beautiful
is Mount Bromo. Dawn breaks over the caldera through dazzling clouds and
mist and Mount Bromo's farmers head for high fields with the firm steps
of lives rooted in the ground. Straightening human spines, despising none,
overwhelmed by nothing, they walk the world.

Sukapura village, Probolinggo, East Java, Indonesia, 2013.

고산 마을의 우체부

높고 멀고 험준한 오지마을에서
세상은 편지로 이어지는 길이다.
저 한 통의 편지 속에 얼마나 많은 사연이,
그리움이, 기쁨과 슬픔이, 애틋함이 담겨 있을까.
몇 날 밤을 쓰고, 고쳐 쓰고, 다시 쓴 편지 한 장.
부친 지 한 달 만에 받아보는 편지를 읽고 또 읽으며
그 거리와 시간만큼 깊어지는 정이 있다.

POSTMAN IN A HIGH MOUNTAIN VILLAGE

In a high, remote, rugged rural village the world is a path linking people through
letters. How many stories are contained in just that one letter. Will it hold longing
or joys, sorrows or affection? One letter, written over several nights, corrected,
rewritten. In reading and rereading a letter just received, posted a month before,
there is a love that grows deeper the greater the distance and time.

On the way to Dongxiangxian, Gansusheng, China, 2012.

A MINER'S PATH

The Pulacayo mine, in mineral rich Bolivia in Latin America. Like Bolivia
itself, the poorest country in South America, long looted by Western capital and
the corruption of the white ruling class, only a few hundred villagers remain
in Pulacayo, living in the traditional way, digging for silver and minerals.
One youthful miner, still cherishing this land though all the others have left,
walks along the bleak path of a miner, like the graves of bygone miners.
His whole body exposed to the scorching sunlight without any shade from
a tree, today, once again, he walks into the underground darkness to dig for
the light of the world above ground.

Pulacayo, Potosi, Bolivia, 2010.

광 부 의 길

중남미의 광물 부국인 볼리비아 풀라까요 광산.
오랜 서구 자본의 수탈과 백인 정권의 부패로
남미에서 가장 가난한 나라가 되고 만 볼리비아처럼
지금 풀라까요에는 수백 명의 주민만이 남아
재래식으로 은과 광물을 캐며 살아가고 있다.
다들 떠나가도 이 땅을 지켜온 청년 광부가
선대 광부들의 무덤만 같은 황량한 광부의 길을 걸어간다.
나무 그늘 하나 없이 온몸으로 불볕을 받으며
오늘도 지상의 빛을 캐러 지하의 어둠 속으로 걸어간다.

카 슈 미 르 의 사 과 나 무 밭

인디아와 파키스탄의 끝나지 않는 분쟁으로
'지상의 낙원'에서 '지옥의 땅'이 되어버린 카슈미르.
길이란 길마다 계엄군의 총칼이 번득이는데
농부는 나무를 돌보러 양 떼를 몰고 나섰다.
"사과나무는 카슈미르의 심장이지요.
   어릴 때부터 이 길을 따라 산 넘고 강 너머까지
   최고의 사과를 전해주었는데….”
사과나무 빈 가지 사이로 바람만 흐른다.

KASHMIR'S APPLE TREE ORCHARDS

Kashmir, transformed from an 'earthly paradise' to a 'land of hell' by the endless
conflict between India and Pakistan. While the weapons of martial law troops
flash along every path, the farmer sets out, driving his sheep on his way to care
for his trees. "The apple tree is the heart of Kashmir. Since I was a child, passing
along this road, over mountains, over rivers, I have delivered the finest apples…."
Only the wind blows between the empty branches of the apple trees.

Srinagar, Jammu Kashmir, India, 2013.

CHILDREN VISITING TREES

The almond tree flowers blooming in Kashmir are the heralds of spring,
announcing the end of long winter. Icy winds still blow but red-cheeked children
pay a visit to the trees. "That's an almond tree planted with Grandfather.
That's a tree that my deceased parents used to like. Tree, tree, come on, bloom,
the sound of our footsteps tells you that we're waiting for you."

On the way to Wagnat village, Jammu Kashmir, India, 2013.

아 이 들 의 '나 무 돌 이'

카슈미르 땅에 피어나는 아몬드나무 꽃은
긴 겨울이 끝났음을 알리는 봄의 전령사다.
아직 언 바람이 불어오는데
붉은 볼의 아이들이 나무돌이를 한다.
"할아버지랑 심은 아몬드나무예요.
돌아가신 엄마아빠가 좋아했던 나무래요.
나무야 나무야 어서어서 꽃 피어라,
우리가 널 이렇게 기다리고 있다고
발자국 소리를 들려주는 거예요."

달 호 수 를 저 어 갈 때

히말라야 만년설이 녹아 흘러 생겨난 달 호수Lake Dal는
아름다운 경관과 선상 시장으로 '동양의 베네치아'라 불린다.
수백 척의 쪽배들이 모여드는 아침 시장이 파하고
다 팔지 못한 과일을 싣고 집으로 돌아가는 길.
"인도군의 계엄령으로 관광객의 발길이 끊겼어요.
분쟁은 끝이 없고 아이들은 저만 바라보는데…."
사내는 카슈미르의 눈물 같은 달 호수를 저어 나간다.

ROWING ACROSS LAKE DAL

Lake Dal, created by the melting of the Himalayan snowfields, is called
'The Venice of the East' because of its beautiful scenery and boat-borne market.
Once the morning market, where hundreds of small boats gather, is over,
they set off back home with the unsold fruit. "Tourists can't visit because of
India's martial law. The conflict is endless and the children just lean on me…."
The man goes rowing across Kashmir's tear-like Lake Dal.

Lake Dal, Jammu Kashmir, India, 2013.

GRANDMA LEFT ALONE

The couple pulled their cart together for so many years. Grandpa passed away first and grandma alone didn't have the strength to pull it alone, but there was a helping hand. Looking at her with a sad face, grandma gave me three oranges and patted my back. 'You who have walked so far, fear nothing. You have suffered enough yet still we have come this far. For those who have lived good, righteous lives, a friend is waiting, even at the very end of the world. Don't lose yourself, don't lose faith, follow your path.'

Jhansi, Uttar Pradesh, India, 2013.

혼자 남은 할머니가

긴긴 세월 부부가 함께 끌어온 수레바퀴.
할아버지가 먼저 세상을 떠나고
할머니 혼자서는 바퀴를 굴릴 힘이 없지만
그래도 도와주는 손길이 있다.
슬픈 얼굴로 바라보는 내게 할머니는
오렌지 세 알을 쥐어주며 등을 토닥인다.
'먼 길을 걸어온 사람아,
아무것도 두려워 마라.
그대는 충분히 고통받아왔고
그래도 우리는 여기까지 왔다.
선하고 의롭게 살아온 이에겐
세상 끝에서도 친구가 기다리니.
자신을 잃지 말고, 믿음을 잃지 말고
그대의 길을 걸어가라.'

아침은 짜이 한 잔

인도의 아침은 짜이 한 잔으로 시작한다.
모닝 짜이를 마시지 않는 아침은 산 날이 아니다.
오늘 하루 인생을 시작하기 전,
깊은 숨을 쉬며 심신을 가다듬는 생의 의례.
아침 태양이 비추는 나무 아래 카페에, 일단 앉아라.
짜이를 마셔라. 인사하라. 한 번 웃어라.
그러면 다른 하루가 시작될 것이니.

IN THE MORNING, A CUP OF CHAI

India's morning starts with a cup of chai. A morning without a morning chai is not a living day. Before starting life today, a ritual of life, taking a deep breath, calming body and soul. Sit down at a cafe beneath a tree shining in the morning sun. Drink chai. Offer greetings. Smile once. Then another day will begin.

Jhansi, Uttar Pradesh, India, 2013.

저 마 다 의 속 도 로

길에서 묻는다.

좋은 길이란 어떤 길인가.

방에서 방으로, 점에서 점으로 가는

최단 거리 길인가.

다양한 생명과 다양한 탈것들이

자기만의 속도와 리듬으로 오가는 길인가.

인간이 추방되고 동물이 추방되고

짐수레와 마차와 자전거와 유모차와

순례자와 내 두 발이 추방된 독점의 길.

좋은 길이 없는 좋은 삶이란 없다.

EACH AT THEIR OWN PACE

On the path, ask: What kind of path is a good path? Is the shortest distance
from room to room, from point to point, a good path? Is it a path where various
lives and various vehicles each move along at their own pace and rhythm?
An exclusive path, one from which people are excluded, animals excluded,
carts, wagons, bicycles, strollers, pilgrims and my two feet are excluded.
There is no good life without a good path.

Auli village, Orissa, India, 2013.

설 레 는 귀 향 길

이슬람 최대 명절인 '이드 알 아드하'를 맞아
거대한 귀향 행렬이 이어진다.
버스 지붕 위까지 빼곡히 앉고 서고 매달린 채로
10시간이 넘고 2박 3일이 넘는 길이지만
이보다 더 즐거운 고행길이 있을까.
한 사람의 인생에서 돌아갈 곳이 있고
돌아갈 사람이 있다는 것은 얼마나 큰 행복인가.
고단한 삶의 무게로 지친 몸과 마음을 회생시켜주고
다시 살아갈 힘을 주는 곳이 있다는 것은
얼마나 큰 축복인가.

THE EXCITEMENT OF RETURNING HOME

To celebrate Eid al-Adha, Islam's biggest holiday, a huge procession of people returning home advances. Densely packed, sitting on the roof of the bus, standing, clinging, it's a journey lasting over ten hours, two nights and three days, but can there be a more pleasant penance in going home? What happiness that there is a place to go back to, and that there is someone going back to each person's life. What a blessing that there is a place that gives strength to go on living, reviving bodies and minds wearied by the weight of a hard life.

Lahore, Punjab, Pakistan, 2011.

CHILD OF A TREE

The history and dignity of a village is a beautiful forest. A person grows deeper with a majestic tree, a tree that has passed through great suffering. Children grow up leaning against such a tree. I am the child of a tree; the tree is my temple. Other children follow walking behind me and trees tell secret stories about life by the whispering of the wind.

Auli village, Orissa, India, 2013.

나무의 아이

한 마을의 역사와 품격은 아름드리 숲이다.
크나큰 고난을 뚫고 온 장엄한 세월의 나무,
그 나무와 함께 사람은 깊어진다.
그 나무에 기대어 아이들은 자란다.
나는 나무의 아이, 나무는 나의 성전.
내 등 뒤에서 또 다른 아이들이 걸어오고
나무들은 무언가 비밀스런 삶의 이야기를
바람의 속삭임으로 전해주리라.

사 랑 의 무 게

묵직한 물 항아리를 이고
날마다 사막을 건너는 라자스탄 여인들.
귀한 물을 기다리는 식구들과 가축들을 위해
무거운 걸음을 하루도 멈출 수 없다.
세상에서 가장 무거운 건 사랑,
사랑 없이 무거운 짐을 지고 갈 수 있을까.
사랑의 무게를 지고 걷는 고귀한 이여.

THE WEIGHT OF LOVE

Carrying heavy water jars on their heads, Rajasthan women cross the desert every day. For the sake of families and livestock waiting for precious water they cannot stop their heavy steps for even a day. The heaviest thing in the world is love. Could they carry such heavy burdens without love? Noble folk, walking along bearing the weight of love.

Jaipur, Rajasthan, India, 2013.

길 위의 학교

먼 길을 걸어 선생님이 찾아온 날,
수업을 듣는 아이들은 마치 활자를
자신의 오장육부에 새기겠다는 듯
빛나는 눈길로 책 속으로 걸어간다.
길 위의 학교에선 안 되는 게 없다.
어깨너머로 배운 동생들이 "저요, 저요!"
언니 오빠를 뛰어넘어 버리고,
막내는 "오늘의 반장은 내가 할래"
배움에 목마른 형과 누나들에게
바지런히 물을 길어다 나르고,
"쌤, 아기 양한테 먹이 주고 올게요,
진도 나가지 마요." 씽 다녀온다.
등 뒤의 벼는 익을수록 고개를 숙이고
아이들은 간절한 만큼 고개를 숙인다.

SCHOOL ON THE ROAD

One day, when the teacher arrived after walking a long way, the children attending class walked into the book with shining eyes as if they were going to engrave every single word on their inner organs. There's nothing you can't do in a school on the road. The younger brothers who learned by watching, saying, "Me, me!" outdid their older sister and brother the youngest insisting, "I want to be today's class captain," he tirelessly provides water to brothers and sisters thirsty to learn. "I'll be back after feeding the lambs. Don't go on studying without me," coming back in a flash. The more the rice behind his back ripens, the more ardent the children, the more they bow.

Sargodha, Punjab, Pakistan, 2011.

안 데 스 의 돌 담

선조들이 쌓아 올린 긴 돌담을 자긍심에 찬
몸짓으로 가리켜 보이는 안데스의 소녀.
이 돌담은 어린 알파카의 울타리가 되어주고
언 바람으로부터 감자 싹을 지켜주고
한낮의 태양을 품어 땅에 이슬을 전해준다.
척박한 곳에서도 최선의 삶을 꽃피우기 위해
대를 이어가며 쌓아 올린 안데스의 돌담은
너는 무얼 쌓아 물려주겠냐고 묻는 것만 같다.

A STONE WALL IN THE ANDES

A girl in the Andes gestures, proud of the long stone walls piled up by her ancestors. This stone wall serves as a fence for the young alpacas, protects the potato shoots from the freezing wind, embraces the midday sun and delivers dew to the ground. The stone walls of the Andes that have been piled up over generations to enable the best life to bloom even in barren places seem to be asking what you will pile up and hand down.

Yanacancha village, Andes Mts., Peru, 2010.

BEYOND THE SNOW-TOPPED MOUNTAINS

The path passes endlessly over the snow-topped mountains. In the cold, thin air,
I grew weary but there is someone who calmly lives here. Life may be about
experiencing the world but it is also about experiencing yourself as a human being.
Just as there is the highest snow-topped mountain in the world, so too everyone
has their own topmost peak. Not for the sake of possessing the experience of the
peak but for the sake of extinguishing oneself in the experience of the peak.
For the sake of a love like those snow-topped mountains, for a heart-aching love.

On the way to Chitral from Shandur Pass, Pakistan, 2011.

만 년 설 산 을 넘 어

넘어도 넘어도 끝없는 만년설산의 길.
춥고 희박한 공기 속에 난 그만 지쳤는데
이곳에서 저리 태연히 살아가는 이가 있다.
인생은 세상을 경험하는 것이지만
인간으로서 자기 자신을 체험하는 것이기도 하다.
지상에는 가장 높은 만년설산이 있듯이
누구나 자신만의 절정의 경지가 있다.
절정의 경험을 소유하기 위해서가 아니라
절정의 체험 속에 자신을 소멸하기 위해.
저 만년설산 같은 사랑, 가슴 시린 사랑을 위해.

코카 잎을 입에 물고

열 걸음만 걸어도 숨쉬기 힘든 안데스 산정에서
알파카를 몰고 가던 께로족 여인이
품속에서 꺼낸 코카 잎 한 줌을 입에 넣어준다.
"이 높은 산정에서 우리가 의지할 것은
이 코카 잎과 파차마마 여신뿐이지요.
코카 잎의 쓰디쓴 맛을 아는 사람만이
인생의 달콤한 순간에 감사하며
다시 일어나 더 높이 걸어갈 수 있지요."

COCA LEAVES IN THE MOUTH

High up in the Andes, where breathing is difficult after even ten steps,
the Q'ero woman driving alpacas takes a handful of coca leaves and puts
them in my mouth. "The only things that we can depend on in these
high mountains are these coca leaves and the goddess Pachamama.
Only one who knows the bitter taste of coca leaves can give thanks for
the sweet moments of life, stand up again and go walking on yet higher."

On the way to Chullupampa village, Andes Mts., Peru, 2010.

맨발의 삼총사

수시로 맹수들이 출몰하는 아프리카 고원에서
연료로 쓸 마른 소똥과 일용할 이삭을 채취해
집으로 돌아가는 맨발의 아이들.
"우리는 늘 셋이서 함께 다녀요.
그러면 짐승을 만나도 무섭지 않아요.
길을 잃어도 머리를 맞대고
무거운 짐도 나눠 드니까요."

BAREFOOT TRIO

On the plateaus of Africa, where many predators roam, barefooted children
return home after gathering dry cow dung for fuel and grains for food.
"We always go around together in threes. Then we are not afraid
if we encounter wild animals. If we get lost, we put our heads together
and we help each other carry heavy loads."

Bahir Dar, Ethiopia, 2008.

A BOUNDLESS DESERT

The vast Nubian Desert stretches east of the Nile. The pyramids are silent, harboring a glorious mystery. Herds of camels cross the scorching desert. Is there anyone who hasn't felt how every turning path of life is like a desert? No matter how far you go, the endless desert is boundless. However, once the boundlessness disappears, it is stifling. Life is a journey cultivating that boundlessness.

Meroe, Nubian, Sudan, 2008.

막막한 사막

나일강 동쪽에 펼쳐진 광대한 누비아 사막.
피라미드는 찬란한 신비를 품고 묵언 중이고
낙타 떼는 불타는 사막을 가로질러 간다.
인생의 어느 고비 길이 사막 같다고
느껴보지 않은 사람이 어디 있을까.
가도 가도 끝이 없는 사막은 막막하여라.
그러나 막막함이 사라지고 나면 숨막힘인 것을.
삶은 그 막막함을 가꿔나가는 여정인 것을.

낙 타 가 간 다

'사막의 배'라 불리는 낙타는
아브라함 시대로부터 오늘날까지
사막과 광야와 고원의 동행자이다.
길 없는 길을 누가 가는가.
낙타가 간다.
자신을 위한 먹이도 물도 없이 누가 가는가.
낙타가 간다.
낙타가 사막의 가시 돋친 낙타초를 씹으며
노을 속에 무릎을 꿇고 먼 곳을 바라볼 때
나 또한 가야만 할 먼 길을 바라본다.

THE CAMEL GOES ON

The camel is called the 'ship of the desert'. Since the days of Abraham until today
they have been traveling companions across desert, wilderness, and plateau.
Who follows a path where there is no path? The camel. Who advances
without food and water for themselves? The camel. As camels chew the desert's
thorny camel grass, kneeling down at sunset and gazing into the distance
I too gaze at the long path that I still have to take.

Axum, Ethiopia, 2008.

내 그리운 '바그다드 카페'

2003년 이라크 전쟁 때 머문 시리아 사막 길의 바그다드 카페.
카페 주인은 전쟁터에 뛰어든 나를 위해 흰 양피지에
자신이 손수 그린 세상에서 한 장뿐인 지도를 내주었다.
이제 이라크와 시리아는 '여행금지국'이 되었다.
갈 수 없고 만날 수 없는 이들은 늘 나를 부르고 있다.
내 그리운 바그다드 카페에서.

MY DEAR 'BAGHDAD CAFE'

Baghdad cafe lies on a desert road in Syria where I stayed during the 2003
Iraq war. After I came rushing to the war zone the owner of the cafe gave me
a map that he drew for me on white parchment, the only one in the world.
Nowadays Iraq and Syria are forbidden travel zones. The people I cannot go to,
cannot meet, are all the time calling me. In my dear Baghdad cafe.

On the way to Baghdad from Palmyra, Syria, 2008.

고립된 팔레스타인

이스라엘은 팔레스타인 땅을 불법점령하고
분리장벽을 세워 모든 길과 길을 끊어놓았다.
팔레스타인 사람들은 자기 땅에 갇힌 수인囚人처럼
학교를 갈 때도 병원과 직장과 친척 집을 갈 때도
총구가 번득이는 긴 감시로를 걸어가야 한다.
인간에게 있어 길을 끊고, 발을 묶고,
서로를 고립시키는 것만큼 큰 죄악이 있을까.

PALESTINE ISOLATED

After Israel illegally occupied Palestine a separation barrier was established,
cutting all roads and paths. The Palestinians are like prisoners, when they go to
school, to hospital, to their workplace, or to a relative's house, they have to walk
along a long surveillance path where guns flash. For human beings, is there any
evil as great as isolating people one from another, cutting paths, binding feet?

Ramallah, Palestine, 2008.

눈 물 흐 르 는 지 구 의 골 목 길 에 서

나는 많은 길을 걸어왔다.

내가 걷는 길은 태양보다 눈물이 더 많았다.

아침부터 찬비가 내린다.

나에게 지구는 하나의 커다란 눈물방울.

젊어서 먼저 생을 완주한 나의 동지들이

폭음 속에서 내 품에 안기던 여윈 아이들이

영혼의 총을 들고 산으로 가던 소녀 게릴라들이

그만 등을 돌리고 싶은 길에서 나를 부르는 소리.

눈물이 길이다. 눈물이 길이다.

눈물은 자신이 가야 할 길을 안다.

눈물이 흐르는 길을 따라가라.

ALONG THE ALLEYS OF WEEPING EARTH

I have come walking along many paths. On the paths I followed, there were more tears than sunlight. It has been cold, raining since morning.
For me, the Earth is one huge teardrop. My comrades whose lives ended first, still young, gaunt children I held in my arms amidst explosions, girl guerrillas who took to the mountain bearing soul guns, voices calling me from paths where I wanted to turn my back. Tears are the path. Tears are the path. Tears know the path they must take. Follow the path where tears flow.

Turkey, 2005.

WHEN THE WIND BLOWS

When the wind blows on the Ethiopian Plateau, the children go running anywhere, anywhere. Running over meadows, running along dirt paths, running over wheat fields. Whether hoping to satisfy their hunger or to find warmth, boy meets girl, friend calls friend. On a windy day, my soul goes running. Anywhere, anywhere, toward you whom I yearn for.

Gondar, Ethiopia, 2008.

바 람 이 불 어 오 면

에티오피아 고원에 바람이 불어오면
아이들은 어디로든, 어디로든 달려 나간다.
초원을 달리고 흙길을 달리고 밀밭을 달린다.
허기를 채우려는지 온기를 찾는 것인지
소년은 소녀를 만나고, 친구는 친구를 부른다.
바람이 부는 날이면 내 영혼은 달려 나간다.
어디로든, 어디로든, 그리운 네가 있는 쪽으로.

베 두 인 소 녀

아프리카 북부 사막에서 유목 생활을 하는 베두인은
핏속에 바람이 들어있어 바람이 부는 곳으로
태양과 별의 지도를 따라 한평생 유랑하며 살아간다.
보아주는 이도 없는 모래먼지 날리는 사막에서
고운 옷차림으로 일을 하던 소녀는
"베두인 여자의 아름다움은요
낙타의 강인함과 풀잎의 온유함이에요."
사막의 초생달 같은 가슴 서늘한 눈빛으로 말한다.
누구든지, 어디에 살든지, 무엇을 하는지,
강건함과 총명함과 다정함이 인간의 기품이 아니겠는가.

A BEDOUIN GIRL

Bedouins live a nomadic life in the deserts of northern Africa. Since they
have the wind in their blood, they spend their lives travelling, following
the map of the sun and the stars. In the desert where sand goes flying, with
none to watch over them, a girl who had been working in fine attire says,
"The beauty of a Bedouin woman is the strength of a camel and the
gentleness of a blade of grass." She speaks with piercing eyes like a desert
crescent moon. Surely, no matter who you are, where you live, what you do,
strength and braininess and kindness are the finest human qualities?

On the way from Kassala to Al Qadarif, Sudan, 2008.

가슴 시린 풍경 하나

"어려서부터 70이 넘도록 야크를 돌보다
늘 여기 앉아 강물을 바라보곤 하지요.
저 흰 산의 눈물이 나를 키워주었지요.
어머니의 눈물이, 죽은 아내의 눈물이,
내 가슴에 흘러 흘러 나를 살게 했지요."
'가슴 시린 풍경' 하나 품고 산다는 것.
'가슴 시린 사람' 하나 안고 산다는 것.

A HEART-WRENCHING VIEW

"I have been caring for yak since I was a child till now I am past seventy.
I always sit here, looking at the river. It was that white mountain's tears that
raised me. My mother's tears, my dead wife's tears, flowing into my heart,
kept me alive." A life cherishing one 'heart-wrenching view.' A life embracing
one 'heart-wrenching person.'

Gilgit, Pakistan, 2011.

사 이 좋 은 형 제

두 아이가 길을 간다.
보고 또 봐도 무슨 이야기가 그리 많은지
작은 새처럼 지저귀며 생기차게 걸어간다.
총성이 울리는 위험 가득한 길이지만
이 길에서는 내가 널 지켜주겠다는 듯
두 살 많은 아이는 동생의 어깨를 감싼다.
혼자서는 갈 수 없다. 웃으며 가는 길이라도.
함께라면 갈 수 있다. 눈물로 가는 길이라도.

BROTHERS IN HARMONY

Two children go walking along a path. They are always together, I wonder
how they can have so much to say. Chirping like little birds, they walk along
briskly. It's a path full of danger, echoing with gunfire but the child two years
older has his arm round his brother's shoulder as if to say, I will protect you
along this path. We cannot go alone. Even on a path we can follow smiling.
We can only go if we are together. Even along a path taken in tears.

Sargodha, Punjab, Pakistan, 2011.

BETWEEN TALL TREES

I wept as I walked between tall trees. For I am too small,
I am too weak, the forest of tall trees is a deep and rugged path
I laughed as I walked between tall trees. For inside me there is
a far bigger, stronger, nobler I than I realized. I understood as
I walked between tall trees. A person who walks between
tall trees brings the forest of tall trees into being.
'As I walked between tall trees, I grew taller.'

Cusco, Peru, 2010.

124

키 큰 나무 사이로

키 큰 나무 사이를 걸으며 나는 울었다.
내가 너무 작아서, 내가 너무 약해서,
키 큰 나무 숲은 깊고 험한 길이어서.

키 큰 나무 사이를 걸으며 나는 웃었다.
내 안에는 내가 생각하는 것보다
훨씬 크고 강하고 고귀한 내가 있었기에.

키 큰 나무 사이를 걸으며 나는 알았다.
키 큰 나무 사이를 걸어온 사람이
키 큰 나무 숲을 이루어간다는 걸.

'키 큰 나무 사이를 걸으니 내 키가 커졌다.'

전쟁의 레바논에서, 박노해. Park Nohae in the battlefield of Lebanon, 2007.

박노해

1957 전라남도에서 태어났다. 16세에 상경해 낮에는 노동자로 일하고 밤에는 선린상고(야간)를 다녔다. **1984** 스물일곱 살에 첫 시집 『노동의 새벽』을 출간했다. 군사독재 정권의 금서 조치에도 100만 부 가까이 발간된 이 시집은 당시 잊혀진 계급이던 천만 노동자의 목소리가 되었고, 대학생들을 노동현장으로 뛰어들게 하면서 한국 사회와 문단을 충격으로 뒤흔들었다. 감시를 피해 사용한 박노해라는 필명은 '박해받는 노동자 해방'이라는 뜻으로, 이때부터 '얼굴 없는 시인'으로 알려졌다. **1989** 분단된 한반도에서 사회주의를 처음 공개적으로 천명한 〈남한사회주의노동자동맹〉(사노맹)을 결성했다. **1991** 7년여의 수배생활 끝에 안기부에 체포되면서 처음으로 얼굴을 드러냈다. 24일간의 고문 후 '반국가단체 수괴' 죄목으로 사형이 구형되고 무기징역에 처해졌다. **1993** 독방에서 두 번째 시집 『참된 시작』을 출간했다. **1997** 옥중에세이 『사람만이 희망이다』를 출간했다. 이 책은 수십만 부가 퍼지며, 그의 몸은 가둘 수 있지만 그의 사상과 시는 가둘 수 없음을 보여주었다. **1998** 7년 6개월의 수감 끝에 석방되었다. 이후 민주화운동 유공자로 복권됐으나 국가보상금을 거부했다. **2000** "과거를 팔아 오늘을 살지 않겠다"며 권력의 길을 뒤로 하고 '생명 평화 나눔'을 기치로 한 비영리 사회운동단체 〈나눔문화〉(www.nanum.com)를 설립했다. **2003** 이라크 전쟁터에 뛰어들면서, 전 세계 가난과 분쟁 현장에서 평화활동을 이어왔다. **2010** 낡은 흑백 필름 카메라로 기록해온 사진을 모아 첫 사진전 「라 광야」展과 「나 거기에 그들처

럼」展(세종문화회관)을 열었다. 304편의 시를 엮어 12년 만의 시집 『그러니 그대 사라지지 말아라』를 출간했다. **2012** 나눔문화가 운영하는 〈라 카페 갤러리〉에서 박노해 사진전을 상설 개최하고 있다. 파키스탄 사진전 「구름이 머무는 마을」, 버마 사진전 「노래하는 호수」, 티베트 사진전 「남김없이 피고 지고」, 안데스 께로 사진전 「께로티카」, 수단 사진전 「나일 강가에」, 에티오피아 사진전 「꽃피는 걸음」, 볼리비아 사진전 「티티카카」, 페루 사진전 「그라시아스 알 라 비다」, 알 자지라 사진전 「태양 아래 그들처럼」, 인디아 사진전 「디레 디레」, 카슈미르 사진전 「카슈미르의 봄」, 인도네시아 사진전 「칼데라의 바람」, 쿠르드 사진전 「쿠르디스탄」, 라오스 사진전 「라오스의 아침」, 팔레스타인 사진전 「올리브나무의 꿈」 그리고 「하루」, 「단순하게 단단하게 단아하게」, 「길」展을 개최했다. 현재 18번째 전시를 이어가고 있으며, 총 30만 명의 관람객이 다녀갔다. **2014** 아시아 사진전 「다른 길」展(세종문화회관) 개최와 함께 사진에세이 『다른 길』을 출간했다. **2017** 『촛불혁명-2016 겨울 그리고 2017 봄, 빛으로 쓴 역사』(감수)를 출간했다. **2020** 첫 번째 시 그림책 『푸른 빛의 소녀가』를 출간했다. 감옥에서부터 30년 동안 써온 단 한 권의 책, '우주에서의 인간의 길'을 담은 사상서를 집필 중이다. '적은 소유로 기품 있게' 살아가는 삶의 공동체 〈참사람의 숲〉을 꿈꾸며, 오늘도 시인의 작은 정원에서 꽃과 나무를 심고 기르며 새로운 혁명의 길로 나아가고 있다.

매일 아침, 사진과 글로 시작하는 하루 〈박노해의 걷는 독서〉 parknohae park_nohae

Park Nohae

1957 Park Nohae was born in South Jeolla Province. Park left his hometown and moved to Seoul when he was 16 years old, he worked during daytime and attended the night classes at Seollin Commercial High School. **1984** Park published his first collection of poems, *Dawn of Labor*, that he wrote at the age of twenty-seven. Nearly a million copies of this collection were sold, in spite of the Korean government's ban, and it shook Korean society and the literary world with its shocking emotional power. This book became the voice representing the forgotten class of ten million workers and encouraged college students to go into the laboring world. He decided to take a pen name, "Park Nohae," meaning "liberation of the laborers," in order to avoid the dictatorial government's surveillance on him. From that time, he was called the "faceless poet." **1989** He formed the "South Korean Socialist Workers' Alliance" that made socialism a public issue for the first time in South Korea. **1991** After more than seven years in hiding he was arrested, and thus finally revealed his 'face.' After twenty-four days of investigation with illegal torture, the prosecution demanded the death penalty for the 'leader of an anti-state organizations,' and he was sentenced to life imprisonment. **1993** While he was in prison, a second poetry collection was published, *True Beginning*. **1997** He published a collection of essays, titled *Only a Person is Hope*. This book sold hundreds of thousands of copies, showing that although his body could be imprisoned, his ideas and poems could not be restrained. **1998** He was finally freed after seven years and six months in prison. Thereafter, he was reinstated as a contributor to the democratization movement, but he refused any state compensation. **2000** Park decided to leave the way for power, saying, "I will not live today by selling the past," and he established a nonprofit social movement organization "Nanum Munhwa," meaning "Culture of Sharing," (www. nanum.com) that would have "Life, Peace, and Sharing" as its core values. **2003** Right after the United States' invasion of Iraq, he flew to the field of war. Since then, he has continued to conduct activities aimed at establishing global peace in places of poverty and conflict. **2010** He held his first photo exhibition, titled "Ra Wilderness," and second exhibition "Like them, I am there" at the Sejong Center for the Performing Arts (one of the most significant culture and arts spaces in Seoul). In October, he published a new collection of poems after twelve years, titled *So You Must Not Disappear*, containing three hundred and four poems. **2012** "Ra Cafe Gallery" that "Nanum Munhwa" runs, has been holding permanent exhibitions of Park Nohae. He continues to hold photo exhibitions, and a total of 300,000 visitors have so far visited his exhibitions. **2014** Park held a photo exhibition on Asia, titled "Another Way," and at the same time published his collection of photo essays with the same title, *Another Way.* **2017** He supervised the publication of a book, *The Candlelight Revolution—History written with light-From winter of 2016 to spring of 2017.* **2020** Park published his first poetry picture book, *The Blue Light Girl.* He is writing a book of reflexions, the only such book he has written during the thirty years since prison, "The Human Path in Space." Dreaming of the Forest of True People, a life-community living "a graceful life with few possessions," the poet is still planting and growing flowers and trees in his small garden, advancing along the path toward a new revolution.

Every morning poem with photo, 'Park Nohae's Reading while Walking' parknohae park_nohae

박노해 저서   Books by Park Nohae

하루 박노해 사진에세이 01

박노해 시인이 지난 20여 년 동안
기록해온 '유랑노트'이자 길 찾는
이들의 가슴에 띄우는 '두꺼운 편지',
「박노해 사진에세이」시리즈. 그 첫
번째 책『하루』가 2019년 출간되었다.
세계의 다양한 하루를 마주하며,
나의 하루에 경이와 선물이 되어줄 책.
"나는 하루 하루 살아왔다. 감동하고
감사하고 감내하며."(박노해)

136p | 18,000KRW | 2019

One Day   Park Nohae Photo Essay 01

One day published in 2019, is the
first volume in the 'Park Nohae
photo essay' series, 'vagabond notes'
and 'thick letters' recorded over
the past twenty years and addressed
to the hearts of all those people
seeking the way. This book enables
you to experience one day across
the world, making your own one
day wonderful and present. "I have
ever lived day by day. I am touched,
give thanks, endure."(Park Nohae)

단순하게 단단하게 단아하게

박노해 사진에세이 02

"최고의 삶의 기술은 언제나 가장
단순한 것으로 가장 풍요로운 삶을
꽃피우는 것이니."(박노해) 결핍과
고난 속에서도 단순한 살림으로
풍요롭고, 단단한 내면으로 희망차고,
단아한 기품으로 눈부시게 살아가는
지구마을 사람들의 일상이 37점의
흑백사진과 이야기로 펼쳐진다.

128p | 18,000KRW | 2020

Simply, Firmly, Gracefully

Park Nohae Photo Essay 02

"Surely, life's finest skills, being
always the simplest, bring a life of
plenty to bloom."(Park Nohae)
Productive in simple living despite
lack and suffering, full of hope,
inwardly robust, gracefully living
dazzling lives, the daily lives of
inhabitants of the Global Village
unfold in thirty-seven black-and-
white photos and texts.

그러니 그대 사라지지 말아라

영혼을 뒤흔드는 시의 정수. 저항과
영성, 교육과 살림, 아름다움과 혁명
그리고 사랑까지 붉디 붉은 304편의
시가 담겼다. 인생의 갈림길에서 길을
잃고 헤매는 순간마다 어디를 펼쳐
읽어도 좋을 책. 입소문만으로 이 시집
을 구입한 6만 명의 독자가 증명하는
감동. "그러니 그대 사라지지 말아라"
그 한 마디가 나를 다시 살게 한다.

560p | 18,000KRW | 2010

So You Must Not Disappear

The essence of soul-shaking poetry!
This anthology of 304 poems as red as
its book cover, narrating resistance, spiri-
tuality, education, living, the beautiful,
revolution and love. Whenever you're lost
at a crossroads of your life, it will guide
you with any page of it moving you.
The intensity of moving is evidenced by
the 60,000 readers who have bought
this book only through word-of-mouth.
"So you must not disappear." This one
phrase makes me live again.

노동의 새벽

1984년, 27살의 '얼굴 없는 시인'이 쓴 시집 한 권이 세상을 뒤흔들었다. 독재 정부의 금서 조치에도 100만 부 이상 발간되며 화인처럼 새겨진 불멸의 고전. 억압받는 천만 노동자의 영혼의 북소리로 울려퍼진 노래. "박노해는 역사이고 상징이며 신화다. 문학사적으로나 사회사적으로 우리는 그런 존재를 다시 만날 수 없을지 모른다."(문학평론가 도정일)

172p | 12,000KRW | 2014
30th Anniversary Edition

The Dawn Of Labor

In 1984, an anthology of poems written by 27 years old 'faceless poet' shook Korean society. Recorded as a million seller despite the publication ban under military dictatorship, it became an immortal classic ingrained like a marking iron. It was a song echoing down with the throbbing pulses of ten million workers' souls. "Park Nohae is a history, a symbol, and a myth. All the way through the history of literature and society alike, we may never meet such a being again."(Doh Jeong-il, literary critic)

사람만이 희망이다

34살의 나이에 '불온한 혁명가'로 무기징역을 선고받은 박노해. 그가 1평 남짓한 독방에 갇혀 7년 동안 써내려간 옥중에세이. "90년대 최고의 정신적 각성"으로 기록되는 이 책은, 희망이 보이지 않는 오늘날 더 큰 울림으로 되살아난다. 살아있는 한 희망은 끝나지 않았다고. 다시, 사람만이 희망이라고.

320p | 15,000KRW | 2015

Only A Person Is Hope

Park Nohae was sentenced to life imprisonment as a "rebellious revolutionary" when he was 34 years old. This essay written in solitary confinement measuring about three sq. m. for seven years. This book is recorded as the "best spiritual awakening in the 90s," is born again with the bigger impression today when there seems to be no hope at all. As long as you live, hope never ends. Again, only a person is hope.

다른 길

"우리 인생에는 각자가 진짜로 원하는 무언가가 있다. 분명, 나만의 다른 길이 있다."(박노해) 인디아에서 파키스탄, 라오스, 버마, 인도네시아, 티베트까지 지도에도 없는 마을로 떠나는 여행. 그 길의 끝에서 진정한 나를 만나는 새로운 여행에세이. '이야기가 있는 사진'이 한 걸음 다른 길로 우리를 안내한다.

352p | 19,500KRW | 2014

Another Way

"In our lives, there is something which each of us really wants. For me, certainly, I have my own way, different from others."(Park Nohae) From India, Pakistan, Laos, Burma, Indonesia to Tibet, a journey to villages nowhere to be seen on the map. And a new essay of meeting true self at the end of the road. 'Image with a story' guide us to another way.

푸른 빛의 소녀가 박노해 시 그림책

저 먼 행성에서 찾아온 푸른 빛의 소녀와 지구별 시인의 가슴 시린 이야기. "지구에서 좋은 게 뭐죠?" 우주적 시야로 바라본 우리 삶의 근본 물음. 다가오는 우주시대를 살아갈 아이들의 가슴에 푸른 빛의 상상력을 불어넣는 신비로운 여정. "우리 모두는 별에서 온 아이들. 네 안에는 별이 빛나고 있어."(박노해)

72p | 19,500KRW | 2020

The Blue Light Girl

The poignant tale of paintings of the Blue Light Girl visiting from a distant planet and a poet of Planet Earth. "What is good on Earth?" The fundamental question of our life seen from a cosmic perspective. A mysterious journey inspiring an imagination of blue light in the hearts of the children who will live in the coming space age "We are all children from the stars. Stars are shining in you."(Park Nohae)

길 박노해 사진에세이 03

2판 1쇄 발행 2020년 12월 29일
초판 1쇄 발행 2020년 9월 1일

사진·글 박노해
편집 김예슬, 윤지영
자문 이기명
번역 안서재
표지 디자인 홍동원 표제 글씨 박노해
아날로그 인화 유철수 4도 흑백분판 유화컴퍼니
제작 윤지혜 홍보 마케팅 이상훈
종이 월드페이퍼 인쇄 경북프린팅
제본 광성문화사 후가공 신화사금박

발행인 임소희
발행처 느린걸음
출판등록 2002년 3월 15일 제300-2009-109호
주소 서울시 종로구 사직로8길 34, 330호
전화 02-733-3773
팩스 02-734-1976
이메일 slow-walk@slow-walk.com
홈페이지 www.slow-walk.com
instagram.com/slow_walk_book

ⓒ 박노해 2020
ISBN 978-89-91418-29-5 04810
ISBN 978-89-91418-25-7 04810(세트)

번역자 안선재(안토니 수사)는 서강대학교 명예교수로
40권 이상의 한국 시와 소설의 영문 번역서를 펴냈다.

The Path Park Nohae Photo Essay 03

Second edition, first publishing, Dec. 29, 2020
First edition, first publishing, Sep. 1, 2020

Photographed and Written by Park Nohae
Edited by Kim Yeseul, Yun Jiyoung
Directed by Lee Ki-Myoung
Translation by Brother Anthony of Taizé
Cover Designed by Hong Dongwon
Handwritten Title by Park Nohae
Photographic Analogue Prints are by Yu Chulsu
Quadtone Separation by UHWACOMPANY
Print Making by Yun Jihye
Marketing by Lee Sanghoon

Publisher Im Sohee
Publishing Company Slow Walking
Address Rm330, 34, Sajik-ro 8-gil, Jongno-gu,
Seoul, Republic of Korea
Tel 82-2-7333773 Fax 82-2-7341976
E-mail slow-walk@slow-walk.com
Website www.slow-walk.com
instagram.com/slow_walk_book

ⓒ Park Nohae 2020
ISBN 978-89-91418-29-5 04810
ISBN 978-89-91418-25-7 04810(SET)

Translator An Sonjae(Brother Anthony of Taizé)
is professor emeritus at Sogang University.
He has published over forty volumes of
translations of Korean poetry and fiction.